ALIEN ENCOUNTERS

Chilling True Stories of The Paranormal

Dr. Julia Sanders

Table of Contents

Introduction

Since the dawn of time humans have recorded strange objects in the sky. From the scribes of Pharaoh Thutmose III in 1440 B.C.E. who recorded seeing fiery disks in the sky to the ancient Greeks, the general Timoleon claimed that when at sea a fiery torch in the sky had guided his fleet safely home, and the Romans, both Livy and Pliny the Elder record strange lights and shapes in the sky, people have looked up and thought "what on earth is that?"

As time has progressed and literacy has become more common reports of sightings in the sky have not only increased but have also become more detailed.

On the 14th of April 1561 as dawn broke above the ancient city of Nuremberg, Germany its bleary eyed residents witnessed what was later described as an "aerial battle". People reported seeing large black triangular objects in the sky along with spheres, cylinders and various other shapes. Some reports claimed that one of the triangles crashed outside the city walls. A German broadsheet newspaper described the event in detail and illustrated it with a woodcut by engraver Hans Glaser.

A series of similar celestial phenomena was reported to have taken place over the skies of Basel, Switzerland in 1566. The Basel pamphlet of 1566, produced by historian Samuel Coccius, described strange sunrises and sunsets while numerous red and black balls fought in the sky. A total eclipse of the moon was also reported. Interestingly while Ufologists regard this as a recorded alien encounter Coccius interpreted it as a religious event.

These types of miracle or sky spectacles were common in the 15th and 16th centuries other notable examples occurred in Wallachia and South Korea.

As our understanding of the night sky and space has grown; many of these sightings have found explanations in the form of stars, planets or meteor showers. Some however are yet to be satisfactorily explained. Throughout the following chapters we will be looking at some of the best known and most intriguing alien encounters from all over the world.

Aurora and Airships across America

During 1896 and 1897 thousands of people of different ages, classes and races reported seeing "airships" in the skies above America. There is some dispute over when the first sighting was occurred. While a sighting in Sacramento California, on the 19th of November 1896, is largely accepted as being the first some argue that an incident occurred a few days earlier in Winnemucca, Nevada. Either way this heralded an important and busy "airship" era. Between late November and early December 1896 the Sacramento Bee and Union and San

Francisco Call reported numerous sightings of these "airships".

By early 1897 the sightings had spread to Washington. Between February and June of that year Texas had become a hot spot for sightings. All the while public interest in the airships was growing. It was against this backdrop that the Aurora encounter occurred.

1897 was not, until this point, the best year for the residents of Aurora, Texas. A devastating fire and a "spotted fever epidemic" had claimed the lives of many of the town's residents while a boll weevil infestation had laid waste to the local cotton crops, the town's main source of revenue. A further blow had come with the construction of a railroad, which, despite initial hopes that it would serve the town, completely bypassed Aurora. For the 3,000 or so residents of Aurora theirs was very much a dying town.

At around 6 a.m. on the 17th of April the citizens who had not given up and moved away, hoping for better times elsewhere were awoken by the appearance of what was described in the local press reports as an "airship". People watched as the craft appeared to malfunction, stalling in the early morning sky before crashing into a windmill on the property of local judge J. S. Proctor. Debris was reportedly scattered over a wide area.

The airship crash was reported in the Morning News, a local newspaper. The article documented that the crafts pilot was also its sole occupant. It went on to describe that "while his remains were badly disfigured" the rescue party and curious onlookers were able to discern that "he was not an inhabitant of this world".

In 1973 United Press International conducted an interview with Mary Evans. At the time of the incident Mary was 15 years of age and was living with her parents in Aurora. Despite her advancing years Mary clearly remembered her parents telling her that the pilot's body had been buried in the town's cemetery. This was common knowledge amongst the townspeople as was the fact that the remains of the craft were disposed of down a nearby well. This is supported by contemporary accounts such as the April the 19th 1897 edition of the Dallas Morning News, which contained a report by Aurora resident S.E. Haydon describing the pilot as being buried with "full Christian rites" in Aurora Cemetery.

Many years later the former Mayor of Aurora Barbara Brammer conducted her own detailed research into the case and concluded that it was probably a hoax. As we have already seen in the months prior to the crash Aurora had suffered a series of tragic incidents and

was in danger of dying out.
Brammer's research found that S. E.
Haydon was a known practical joker.
She came to the conclusion that the
crash and subsequent reports of a
funeral was Haydon's attempt to keep
the town alive.

This theory is supported by the fact
that the Dallas Morning News never
pursued the story further or allowed
S.E. Haydon to write a follow up
detailing, for example, the pilots
funeral. Further enforcing the idea that
the Aurora encounter was a hoax a
1979 article in Time magazine by Etta
Pegues claimed that Judge Proctor
never had a windmill on his property.

More recent investigations into the case have focused on disproving the claims of sceptics. Recent investigations have shown that there was a structure on the Proctor property, not a windmill but a three-storey water pump. Possibly the two may have been confused over time or it may, at one point, have housed a windmill as well.

As for the craft in the well, today there is no trace. If it was ever there unwitting owners probably removed it in the intervening years. However tests on water in the well have shown that the while the water is normal it does contain large amounts of aluminum.

In 1973 the Mutual UFO Network undertook an exploration of Aurora Cemetery. In the grounds they uncovered many unmarked graves one of which was supposedly marked with a strange UFO shaped marker. The team's metal detector gave off a series of interesting readings from the grave. Permission to exhume the grave was denied.

Later it was reported that the marker had been removed and a three-inch pipe had been placed in the ground. The team's metal detector no longer gave off readings from the grave suggesting that whatever was there had been removed.

Over time many of the cases reported during the 1896/ 1897 airship flap have been explained away as practical jokes, balloons, kites, hysteria or planets and stars mistakenly identified. For many the Aurora encounter sits in this category. For others Aurora is the first properly documented interaction with an alien species and the actions of the townspeople in quickly destroying or burying the evidence has hampered it from being taken as seriously as it deserves.

Whatever the truth of Aurora it is undeniably unusual when considered amongst the wider context of the 1896/ 1897 "airship" flap in that it is one of the few cases which actually involved alien contact. Today Aurora is proud of its alien encounter hosting an annual festival, which helps to keep the town alive.

Roswell

Over the years numerous books, films and documentaries have been made attempting to explain the events that occurred at Roswell, New Mexico. What follows here is a basic explanation of the facts followed by an explanation of how the event became embedded in the world psyche.

What was later characterized as "the UFO Wave of 1947" began with 16 alleged sightings that occurred between May the 17th and July the 12th, 1947, (although some researchers claim there was as many as 800 sightings during that period). Interestingly, the "Roswell Incident" was not considered one of these 1947 events until the 1978-1980 time frame.

Roswell is a city located on the High Plains in southeastern New Mexico. From 1941 to 1967 Roswell was home to the Walker Air Force Base also known as Roswell Army Air Field.

In 1947 W.W. "Mac" Brazel was a 48-year-old rancher working the J.B. Foster ranch, 30 miles south east of Corona, New Mexico. On the 14th of June Brazel, accompanied by his 8 year old son Vernon, was around 8 miles from the ranch house when he came across an area of wreckage about 200 yards wide. The debris appeared to consist of rubber strips, tinfoil, paper and sticks. As Brazel was in a hurry to finish his rounds he didn't pay too much attention to it at the time.

When later asked about the size of the craft Brazel was unable to offer any firm answers as he did not see it fall from the sky and did not see it before it was torn up. He therefore had no idea what size or shape it might have been. When pushed for an estimate Brazel suggested that "it might have been about as large as a table top". The balloon which held it up, if that was how it worked, Brazel estimated as being about 12 feet long. Brazel described the rubber as being smoky grey in color.

After reading in the newspapers about the "UFO wave" Brazel began to wonder if he had found the remains of a craft. Accompanied once again by his son Vernon along with his wife and 14-year-old daughter Betty, Brazel returned to the crash site to gather up the debris. While some accounts suggest that the family returned to the site a day or two later others place it as late as July the 4th.

When it was all collected the tinfoil, paper, tape, and sticks made a bundle about three feet long and 7 or 8 inches thick. The rubber sat in a separate pile, which was 19 inches long and 8 inches thick. Brazel estimated that the entire lot weighed about five pounds.

The family found no sign of metal in the area and also found nothing, which may have served as a propeller although at least one paper fin had been glued onto some of the tinfoil. There were no marks showing ownership or any form of writing on any of the wreckage however some tape decorated with flowers was found. While no strings or wires were found some of the paper had eyelets in it, which suggested that some sort of attachment might have been used.

Brazel had previously found weather balloons on the ranch. He was sure that this wreckage was not a weather balloon.

While Brazel did discuss his find with friends in the nearby town of Corona it wasn't until the following Monday, when he was in Roswell on business, that the authorities were informed. Here Brazel approached sheriff George Wilcox and informed him that he thought he had found a flying disk. Wilcox duly passed on the information to Roswell Army Air Field.

An intelligence officer from the base, Major Jesse A Marcel, and a "man in plain clothes"accompanied Brazel to his home to view the debris. Brazel later reported that despite the men's attempts to reconstruct it they were unable to satisfactorily piece the craft back together. Marcel and the man then took the debris back to Roswell Army Air Field.

Early on Tuesday, July the 8th the Roswell Army Air Field issued a press release reporting that "the intelligence office of the 509th bomb group of the Eighth Air Force, Roswell Army Air Field, was fortunate enough to gain possession of a disk".

Also on the 8th of July a telex message was sent to an FBI official from Fort Worth, Texas. It quoted a Major from the Eighth Air Force, based in Fort Worth at Carswell Air Force Base who described the disk as being "hexagonal in shape" and "suspended from a balloon by a cable". The balloon was estimated to be twenty feet in diameter. The message continued to say that Major Curtan thought the object "resembled a high altitude weather balloon with a radar reflector."

As the explosive press release circulated Colonel W. H. Blanchard, commanding officer of the 509th, contacted General R. M. Ramey of the Eighth Air Force in Fort Worth Texas and ordered that the object be flown to Fort Worth Army Air Field. There Warrant Officer Irving Newton identified the object as a weather balloon with a radar reflector. A second press release, this time from Fort Worth, corrected the original statement confirming the object as a weather balloon.

This seemed to settle the matter and Roswell remained largely forgotten until the 1970s. Between 1978 and 1994 UFO researchers including, Stanton T. Friedman, William Moore and Karl T. Pflock along with the team of Kevin D. Randle and Donald R. Schmitt interviewed several hundred people who claimed to have a connection with the events at Roswell in 1947. These interviews were supplemented with many documents obtained via the Freedom of Information Act and others such as Majestic 12, which was supposedly leaked by insiders. Their conclusion was that at least one spacecraft had crashed near Roswell and the government had covered up the incident as well as the recovery of alien bodies.

This pronouncement sparked the publication of numerous contradictory accounts of Roswell by a variety of authors citing a variety of sources. Numerous locations for the crash were presented as were the number of crafts and aliens involved. This was soon supplemented by numerous movies and documentaries, such as Robert Stack's Unresolved Mysteries, which devoted a large portion of one episode to a "recreation" of the Roswell encounter. All of which fuelled the growing belief that an alien craft had crashed at Roswell and that the U.S. Government had covered it up.

Today the events that occurred on the J.B. Foster ranch in 1947 have been exaggerated to the point of almost mythic levels. The seemingly small pile of debris originally recovered is now believed to be a great amount of debris from an ever-expanding area. Similarly the material recovered has evolved from sticks, paper and tinfoil to exotic materials complete with hieroglyphics.

Currently most Roswell believers agree that there were two crash sites and that at the second site alien bodies (the number of which no one agrees on) were found. The recovered wreckage along with the bodies was taken back to Roswell Army Air Field under tight security. Some cite the seemingly sudden development of technologies such as fiber optics as the U.S. Government exploiting and reverse engineering recovered alien technology.

In response to the growing clamour around Roswell an internal investigation was launched by the United States Air Force. The results were summarized in two reports. The first from 1994 concluded that the material recovered was debris from Project Mogul a military surveillance program using high- altitude balloons.

The second report, from 1997, concluded that reports of bodies being recovered were a mixture of anthropomorphic dummies used in various military projects and a combination of people misremembering events, hearsay and hoaxes. Those who believe that alien bodies were recovered from Roswell claim that this is disinformation.

Despite the vast amounts of research and claims of credibility that have arisen surrounding Roswell the fact is much of this evidence is based on verbal accounts. Although there is no firm evidence that a UFO crashed at Roswell, many still believe that what occurred on the ranch outside Corona was a government conspiracy. B. D. Gildenberg has called the Roswell incident "the world's most famous, most exhaustively investigated, and most thoroughly debunked UFO claim". This hasn't stopped Roswell becoming a Mecca for UFO hunters.

Kenneth Arnold

A second notable incident that occurred during the 1947 "UFO wave" was the Kenneth Arnold encounter.

Kenneth Arnold was born on the 29th of March 1915 in Sebeka Minnesota. He spent much of his childhood in Scobey, Montana before attending the University of Iowa. At the time of his encounter Arnold had been employed by the Great Western Fire Control Supply in Boise, Idaho for seven years. This job took Arnold all around the Pacific Northwest and he often flew between destinations.

A skilled and experienced pilot Arnold had clocked over 9,000 flying hours almost half of which were devoted to Search and Rescue Mercy Flyer causes. In short Arnold was a respected businessman and experienced aviator; he bore all the hallmarks of a reliable witness.

On the 24th of June 1947 Arnold was flying a CallAir A-2 from Chehalis, Washington to Yakima, Washington. Arnold had made a brief detour from his original route after learning of a $5,000 reward for the discovery of a U.S. Marine Corps C-46 transport plane, which had crashed near Mount Rainier.

The skies were completely clear and there was a light wind. Just after 3:00 p.m. at about 9,200 feet near Mineral, Washington Arnold gave up his search and started to head east for Yakima. It was then that he saw a bright flashing light, similar to sunlight reflecting in a mirror. Arnold, worried another aircraft was close to him, scanned the skies but could only see a DC-4 around 15 miles away.

Around 30 seconds after that first flash of light Arnold saw a series of bright flashes in the distance to his left, north of Mount Rainier, around 20 to 25 miles away. Realizing that these were not just reflections in his aeroplane's windows Arnold began to watch the objects. He would later describe them as flying in a long chain like a flock of geese.

Thinking they may be a new type of jet Arnold studied them for a tail or other telltale signs. He could find none. The objects, nine in total, seemed dark in profile against the snow covered backdrop of Mount Rainier. Occasionally they gave off a bright light.

At times Arnold said that they seemed so thin and flat that they were practically invisible. Their movement was akin to a saucer skimming across the water. He estimated their angular size as slightly smaller than the distant

DC-4, possibly about the width between the outer engines- around 60 feet.

Arnold would later revise this estimate, realizing that the objects would have to be quite large for him to see any details at that distance. After comparing notes with a United Airlines crew that had experienced a similar sighting 10 days later, he placed the absolute size as larger than a DC-4 airliner (or greater than 100 feet in length). Army Air Force analysts would later estimate 140 to 280 feet.

Arnold watched as the crafts, which stretched out over a distance of around 5 miles, moved on a more or less level horizontal plane weaving from side to side "like the tail of a Chinese kite". He estimated that they reached speeds of around 1200 miles an hour- much faster than the P-80 jets of the time. The encounter left Arnold with an eerie feeling but he suspected it was probably a test flight of a new aircraft.

Landing in Yakima at about 4:00 p.m. Arnold told Al Baxter the airport general manager of his encounter and soon the entire airport staff had heard the story. As Arnold continued on to an air show in Pendleton, Oregon he was unaware that someone at the airport in Yakima had telephoned on head to tell them his story.

On landing Arnold found that his story preceded him. He spent a while discussing his encounter in detail with pilot friends. Some suggested that he had seen some form of guided missile. Despite earlier thinking of similar solutions Arnold was not entirely satisfied with any of these possible explanations.

The next day, June the 25th, reporters interviewed Arnold at the offices of the East Oregonian in Pendleton. They found Arnold to be a reliable witness and his detailed story left many convinced that he was telling the truth. Interestingly it was from these interviews that the term "flying saucer" originated.

As Arnold's story spread around America the man himself quickly grew tired of his newfound fame. He complained that a preacher had told him the crafts were harbingers of doom and that one lady had run screaming from a cafe when he entered. Despite his distaste for celebrity the interviews kept on coming and on the 7th of July two stories were printed in which Arnold suggested that the crafts were of extraterrestrial in origin.

One of the many consistencies in Arnold's story is that throughout all his interviews he always insisted that if the craft weren't of military origin then they were extraterrestrial.

Aside from being a credible witness with a consistent story another factor in the Kenneth Arnold encounter being one of the most credible ever recorded is the amount of supporting testimony from numerous, unconnected individuals. A prospector named Fred Johnson was on Mount Adams at the time of Arnold's flight and reported seeing similar crafts to Arnold. L. G. Bernier of Richland, Washington wrote to the Oregon Journal on July 4th claiming to have seen strange objects over Richland heading towards Mount Rainier. Also in Richland, Ethel Wheelhouse reported seeing flying disks at about the same time as Arnold's sighting.

An investigation by military intelligence in early July found yet another witness- a member of the Washington State forest service who had been on fire watch at a tower in Diamond Gap, 20 miles south of Yakima. This person saw "flashes" at 3:00 pm on the 24th over Mount Rainier. Similarly Sidney B. Gallagher in Washington State also reported seeing shiny disks flashing in the sky. Altogether there were at least 16 reports of UFOs in the Washington State area on that day. However the pilot of the DC-4 that Arnold reported as being in his vicinity at the time saw nothing unusual.

The military investigation conducted by Lt Frank Brown and Capt. William Davidson of Hamilton Field, California interviewed Arnold on July 1st. They concluded that Arnold was a credible witness and was not making up his encounter. Formally, however, the Army Air Force insisted that Arnold had seen a mirage.

Later, a second secret investigation by Army Air Force Intelligence with the FBI looked at some of the best UFO sightings, the Kenneth Arnold encounter included. They concluded that the sightings were not imaginary or adequately explained by any known natural phenomena.

Sceptics have argued that what Arnold and the others saw was either a mirage or meteors. Some have even suggested the objects were Pelicans. Ufologists and supporters of Arnold have refuted all these theories.

During a 1950 interview with journalist Edward R. Murrow, Arnold claimed to have seen similar objects on three other occasions and suggested that other pilots in the northwestern region of the U.S. had seen similar things. Until his death in 1984 Arnold maintained that if the objects he had seen were not made by the science of the American military then they must have been of extraterrestrial origin.

The McMinnville Photographs

On the evening of May the 11th 1950, having just fed the rabbits Evelyn Trent was making her way back to the family farmhouse just outside Sheridan, Oregon. As she neared the farmhouse Evelyn happened to glance up at the sky. Despite the day drawing to a close it was still fairly light. Light enough for Evelyn to clearly see a strange metallic disk-shaped object hovering in the sky

As the craft made its way silently across the northeastern sky Evelyn watched its progress. Realizing that she had never seen anything like this before Evelyn called for her husband to come out of the farmhouse to look at the disk. Like his wife Paul Trent was also unable to identify it.

Later the Trents would estimate that the object was around 30 feet in diameter and around quarter of a mile away from where they were standing. It did not spin; instead it appeared to glide, creating a breeze as it moved through the air. The craft was completely silent and neither could see any sign of life.

Despite being mesmerized by the strange object Paul eventually remembered that he had a camera inside the farmhouse. Hurrying to retrieve it he briefly left Evelyn alone to watch the craft. Quickly Paul returned with his Roamer camera and was able to take a photograph.

As Paul fumbled with the camera's cumbersome controls the craft tipped slightly before slowly accelerating to the west. As it did so Paul managed to take a second photograph. From inside the farmhouse Paul Trent's father claimed to have also briefly seen the object before it flew away. The Trents estimated that the encounter lasted for about half an hour in total.

In the days before digital photography the Trents didn't see Paul's photographs immediately. Almost a month had passed by the time the film was finally developed. While they waited the Trents didn't discuss their sighting with anyone outside the family for fear of being ridiculed or not taken seriously.   When the film was developed the couple was relieved to see that the two photographs showed exactly what they had seen that evening- a strange craft floating through the sky.

Emboldened by the photographic evidence Paul casually mentioned the incident to his banker Frank Wortmann. Wortmann was intrigued enough to display the photographs in his bank's window in McMinnville. As a result of Wortmann's actions the photographs soon came to the attention of the local newspaper the Telephone-Register. (Today the paper operates under the name News-Register.)

The editor of the newspaper dispatched reporter Bill Powell to the Trent farm to interview the couple. Powell interviewed Paul and Evelyn separately but heard the same story from them both. He also borrowed the negatives to the pictures. Subsequently on June the 8th the Telephone-Register ran both photographs on its front page alongside a headline proclaiming "At Long Last- Authentic Photographs of Flying Saucer [?]".

As public interest in the photographs grew the story was picked up by International News Service (INS) and circulated to other newspapers around America. On the 26th of June 1950 Life magazine published cropped versions of the photographs alongside a photograph of Paul Trent and his camera.

It was around this time that the negatives to the photographs were lost. While Life magazine had promised the Trents that they would be returned they informed the Trents that the negatives had been misplaced. In 1967 the negatives were found in the files of the United Press International (UPI) news service- UPI and INS had merged in the intervening years.

Instead of being returned to the Trents the negatives were then loaned to Dr William K. Hartmann. Hartmann was an astronomer who, at the time, was employed as an investigator for the Condon Committee- a government funded UFO research project based at the University of Colorado Boulder. Around the same time Hartmann interviewed the Trent family and concluded that they were sincere and didn't seem to be making up their story. Indeed the Trents had never received any money from the photographs and Hartmann could find no evidence that this was a publicity stunt concocted by the couple.

In Hartmann's analysis he concluded that "This is one of the few UFO reports in which all factors investigated geometric, psychological, and physical, appear to be consistent with the assertion that an extraordinary flying object, silvery, metallic, disk-shaped, tens of meters in diameter, and evidently artificial, flew within sight of two witnesses."

It was only after Hartmann had finished his investigation and returned the negatives to the UPI did they inform the Trents that the negatives had been rediscovered. In 1970 the

Trents asked Philip Bladine, then editor of the News- Register, for the return of the negatives. While Bladine received the negatives back from the UPI he never passed them onto the Trents. In 1975 Bruce Maccabee an optical physicist for the US Navy and Ufologist discovered the negatives in the files of the News- Register, after conducting his own study of the negatives Maccabee finally returned them to the Trents.

During the 1980s Philip J. Klass and Robert Sheaffer, journalists and sceptics, conducted their own research into the case and concluded that it was a hoax. They argued that that the shadows in the photographs were inconsistent for the time of day they were taken. Klass and Sheaffer theorized that the object was likely a model hanging from power lines visible at the top of the photographs. This led to Hartmann withdrawing his positive assessment of the case.

Despite the work of Klass and Sheaffer, Maccabee remains firm in his assessment that the photographs show a "real physical" object in the sky. He argued that the cloud conditions at the time accounted for the inconsistent shadows. Maccabee believed that the analysis he had done on the negatives showed that the "sighting lines did not cross under the wires" and as Klass and Sheaffer did not account for this he was unconvinced by their argument.

The McMinnville photographs are among the best publicized in UFO history. While sceptics and believers continue to argue over the images authenticity both Paul and Evelyn Trent went to their graves insisting that the encounter was genuine. Today McMinnville is home to America's second largest UFO festival after Roswell.

Kelly-Hopkinsville Encounter

Kelly is little more than a smattering of houses a couple of miles north of Hopkinsville in Christian County, Kentucky. The surrounding area is green and flat with ploughed fields dominating the landscape broken intermittently by clusters of green trees.

Up until the events of the 21st of August 1955 the Sutton family of Kelly, would have been described as a "typical Kentucky family."

Glennie Lankford (50) was the widowed matriarch of the family. It was she who rented the farmhouse that the family lived in. Glennie's two sons from her first marriage, Elmer "Lucky" Sutton (25) and John Charley "J.C." Sutton (21), as well as their respective wives, Vera (29) and Alene (21), and Alene's brother O.P. Baker were with her in the house that night as were Glennie's children from her second marriage: Lonnie (12), Charlton (10) and Mary (7). In addition to the Sutton tribe Billy Ray Taylor (21) and his wife June Taylor (18) were on hand to witness events. The Taylors like Lucky and Vera Sutton were itinerant carnival workers.

At about seven o'clock that evening as Billy Ray Taylor had gone to draw water from the well when he saw a bright light streaking across the evening sky, disappearing beyond a tree line somewhere in the distance. Taylor excitedly returned to the farmhouse to tell the others what he had seen. Unsurprisingly Taylor's claims to have seen a UFO were not taken seriously by the Suttons, who thought a shooting star or meteor a far more likely explanation.

As the families settled down for the night Taylor's story seemed forgotten. Around an hour later the frantic barking of the family dog rudely disturbed them. Hearing other strange noises from outside and assuming that there were intruders on the property

Lucky grabbed his shotgun.
Accompanied by Billy Ray, Lucky
Sutton went outside to investigate.

As they scanned the tree line for signs
of intruders Lucky and Billy Ray saw
something moving. They watched
dumbstruck as the first of the
creatures emerged from the trees.
Lucky took aim but as quickly as he
could shoot at it another would appear
elsewhere. The creatures seemed
impervious to the bullets from Lucky
Sutton's shotgun. When one did
appear to have been hit it would float
to the ground before disappearing.

Lucky and Billy Ray retreated back
inside the farmhouse. Along with

Lucky's brother J.C. and O.P. Baker they claimed to have gone through box after box of ammunition as they vainly tried to quell the unrelenting tide of creatures. Meanwhile the women encouraged the children to hide under their beds before taking shelter themselves.

The terrifying onslaught continued for the next three hours. At times a face would appear at the window only to be greeted with a hail of bullets. On other occasions the creatures appeared to be on the roof looking for a way inside. Once, when the men were brave enough to venture outside, Taylor felt his hair being grabbed by a huge claw like hand.

Eventually, worried that the men may kill each other, Glennie Lankford managed to calm the situation. With everyone able to think more clearly the families decided that the best option was to make a run for it.

The officer on duty at Hopkinsville Police Station had probably been expecting a quiet night, after all nothing much ever happens in rural Kentucky. It was a warm summers night as the clock struggled lazily to the hour- eleven o'clock. The silence of the night was suddenly shattered by the sound of cars being driven at speed. The screeching of tires outside the police station suggested that the officer's night was about to be disturbed.

A group of eleven desperately worried people hurried into the police station. They were all highly agitated and clearly afraid. To the surprise of the bewildered officer the group desperately begged for help claiming to have been "fighting them for nearly four hours".

The officer did his best to calm the group down before they told him their story. Lucky Sutton and Billy Ray Taylor claimed to have been shooting at "twelve to fifteen" short dark figures that had repeatedly "popped up in the doorway or peered in through the windows". While the police were reluctant to believe that aliens had landed they were concerned that the local citizens had been engaged in a shootout. Four city police, five state troopers, three deputy sheriffs and four military police from the nearby US Army Fort Campbell were all dispatched to the Sutton's farmhouse.

Upon inspecting the property they found substantial evidence of gunfire-spent cartridges along with numerous holes in windows and door frames however they found no trace of the little creatures that had supposedly plagued the family. They also found no trace of the UFO landing that Billy Ray Taylor had claimed to see.

With the family calmed and reassured the law enforcement and army left the premises suggesting they should go to bed. When the officers returned the next day they found no sign of the families. Neighbors told them that they had "packed up and left" for Evansville, Indiana after the creatures had returned around 3:30 in the morning. Long before the Suttons reached Indiana their story was becoming a part of local folklore.

Unsurprisingly the attack on the Sutton property received widespread coverage in both the local and national press. Throughout the coverage the description of the creatures seems to vary. They ranged in size from two feet to four feet while they are only described as "little green men" in later accounts. Details such as pointed ears, claw like hands and yellow glowing eyes seem to vary from depending on which report you read.

The inconsistencies in the story and lack of physical evidence have led many to question the veracity of the Kelly-Hopkinsville encounter. Some have speculated that the aliens were in fact Great Horned Owls and that a form of hysteria led to the Suttons and Taylors getting carried away. A meteor shower that was reported at the time could account for Billy Ray Taylors UFO.

Defenders of the Kelly Hopkinsville case claim that the creatures were possibly gremlins or goblins and argue that the number of witnesses involved and the extended length of time over which the encounter occurred point to it being something more than territorial owls. Either way the official investigations never recorded a hoax, simply marking the case as unexplained.

Despite the many doubts the Kelly-Hopkinsville encounter has become firmly lodged in popular culture. The town of Kelly holds an event entitled the Kelly "Little Green Men" Days on the third weekend every August. While numerous books and films have been inspired by the case- the 1986 film Critters is one such example.

Whatever really occurred that night be it a meteor and a pair of territorial owls or little green men from outer space the legend of the Kelly Hopkinsville encounter continues to grow.

Antonio Vilas Boas

The 1950's saw a spate of UFO
sightings all over the world. One of the
most interesting cases of this so-called
"UFO Flap" is that of Antonio Vilas
Boas.

On the family farm in Sao Francisco it
was not unusual for 23-year-old
Antonio Vilas Boas to work through
the night such was the heat of the day.
The night of October the 16th 1957 was
one such night. From his vantage point
in one of the fields Boas could clearly
see a bright red star in the night sky.

Boas stopped his work to watch the
light. This wasn't the first unusual

light to have been seen at the farm. For the previous two weeks both Boas and his brother had noticed a bright light in the sky.

Boas watched motionless, as the "star" seemed to grow larger. After a moment he realized it was heading straight for him. Too afraid to move Boas watched as the light grew in size revealing an egg shaped craft with a red light at its front and a rotating cupola on top. Three spidery legs extended from the craft as it landed in the field.

At this point Boas decided to flee. As he attempted to do so the engine on his tractor died. When Boas attempted to escape on foot a five-foot humanoid in grey coveralls and a helmet seized him. Boas later described its eyes as being small and blue while it spoke in a series of barks or yelps. Three similar humanoids appeared from the craft and aided the first in subduing the farmer before taking him inside.

Once inside the craft Boas was better able to observe his captors. They all wore a "tight-fitting siren-suit" which appeared to have been made of an unevenly striped, grey material. These suits reached all the way up their necks. There they seemed to be joined to a helmet that was made of a grey material "that looked stiffer and was strengthened back at nose level." The helmets obscured everything except the humanoids eyes, which were protected by glasses.

Boas thought that the height of the humanoids helmets suggested that their heads were either twice the size of a normal, human head or that there was something else hidden beneath them. From the helmets came three silvery tubes, Boas was unsure what these tubes were made of. One tube was located in the middle of the helmet; the other two tubes were on either side of the helmet. From there the tubes ran into the humanoids suits: the center tube into a spot where the backbone is while the two side tubes slotted in "under the shoulders at

about four inches from the armpits".
Boas was unsure how these tubes were
attached and could not work out their
purpose.

The room Boas found himself in was
small and square. There were no
furnishings and it was brightly lit,
Boas compared it to "broad daylight".
The light came from recessed square
lights in the smooth metallic walls. An
opening appeared in, what had
appeared to Boas, a seamless wall and
the humanoids led Boas through it
into another room.

Unlike the first this room was
furnished. An oddly shaped table
stood at one side of the room and was

surrounded by several chairs. All were made from the same white metal.

The humanoids grabbed Boas before starting to undress him. Despite Boas' protests he was powerless to stop them. Once naked Boas was rubbed all over with a "thick, clear odorless liquid" before being taken to a third room.

As Boas entered this room he noticed the door had a series of red hieroglyphic like inscriptions on it. Two of the humanoids proceeded to take a blood sample from Boas' chin. This left a series of small scars; when Boas was later examined Doctors recorded these marks.

Boas was left sitting on a featureless "foam rubber like" grey bed in the middle of this room for about half an hour. During this period Boas described how a gas was pumped into the room from holes above his head. This gas, while quick to dissolve, left Boas feeling nauseated as if he was being suffocated. After being sick in a corner of the room Boas found his breathing eased.

A while later a naked woman entered the room. She had long, peroxide blonde hair and big blue eyes. She didn't wear makeup and had very high cheekbones, which gave the impression of a pointed face. Her lips were thin to the point of being invisible.

Boas noted that she was thin and short, possibly only reaching up to his shoulder. Her skin was white but her arms were freckled. While her hair was blonde her pubic and underarm hair was bright red.

Boas claimed that they would spend an hour together engaging in various sexual acts before the woman finally pulled away. Curiously during this encounter the woman declined to kiss Boas, preferring instead to nip his chin. When the deed was done they were joined by one of the original humanoids who took the woman away. Before leaving Boas described her as rubbing her belly before pointing up to the sky. Boas took this to mean that she was now pregnant and intended to raise their child in space.

Boas' clothes were returned to him before he was taken back through the craft. Feeling calmer Boas was now more able to take notice of his surroundings. He described the walls as being smooth and metallic, there appeared to be no windows.

Whilst in what appeared to be the control room Boas noticed a box with a glass top that had the appearance of a clock. It had one hand and marks that would correspond to the placing of numbers on a clock. Boas attempted to take the clock as a memento of his encounter but was prevented from doing so by one of the humanoids.

Boas was taken on a tour of the craft, which he was later able to describe in great detail. The tour complete one of the humanoids led him to a ladder, which descended into the field below the craft. As soon as he was clear of the craft Boas turned and watched as it rose up, its tripod legs retracting, before disappearing into the sky.

By the time Boas returned to his tractor it was around 5:30 in the morning. He estimated that he had spent over four hours in the company of the humanoids.

In the weeks after his encounter Boas suffered from nausea and weakness as well as developing headaches and lesions on the skin. It was during this period that he contacted a journalist by the name of Jose Martins who was known to be interested in UFOs. Upon hearing Boas story Martins contacted Dr Olavo Fontes from the National School of Medicine of Brazil. Fontes like Martins had an interest in UFO cases.

Fontes examined the farmer and concluded Boas was suffering from mild radiation sickness after being exposed to large doses of radiation. That Boas was able to recall his encounter in detail, without the need for any form of hypnotic regression, impressed both Fontes and Martins.

Interestingly while the Boas encounter first came to light in February 1958 it didn't gain much traction in the press until the early 1960s.

When the attention did come Boas quickly became disheartened, feeling that his was a credible story undeserving of all the criticism and skepticism it received. Some sceptics claimed that Boas had invented his encounter, borrowing details from other reported cases to make his own story more believable. Boas soon withdrew from public life to complete his studies and qualify as a lawyer. Throughout his life Antonio Villas Boas stuck to the story of his alien encounter.

Mindalore

Our next story takes place in the closed society of apartheid era South Africa. The mining city of Krugersdorp can be found in the West Rand; around 45 minutes' drive from Johannesburg. It was here, in the suburb of Mindalore that the Quezet family lived.

On the night of January the 3rd 1979 Mrs. Meagan Quezet was sitting in her lounge trying to finish the book she had been reading. As the clock approached midnight her twelve-year-old son Andre entered the room unable to sleep. While Andre made them both a cup of tea Meagan became aware that the family dog, Cheeky, was barking outside. Realizing that Cheeky was loose in the street, and afraid that he would be hit by a car, Meagan called Andre to help her catch the dog.

The Quezet property was located roughly in the middle of Saul Jacobs Street. Meagan and Andre walked along the street towards its junction with Tindall Road. Beyond Tindall Road, around 12 meters further up, is a second road, Chamdor Road. This had been built as a connecting link between the factories in Chamdor and the Lupaardivel Industrial area and was not connected to the lower Tindall Road. Chamdor Road was mainly used by heavy, industrial traffic during the day, at night very little traffic used the route.

When they reached Tindall Road, Meagan and Andre saw Cheeky along with most of the neighbourhood dogs barking frantically at a bright pink light on the higher Chamdor Road. Meagan thought that a light aircraft had come down on the road- the light seemed to be too high above the road to be a police car or any other sort of vehicle. As a nurse Meagan felt duty bound to see if she could help. With this in mind the pair continued up to the top road, making their way over a patch of uneven, overgrown grass before clambering up an embankment.

The nearer that Meagan and Andre got the more obvious it became that the light didn't belong to a plane. Despite being cloaked in a very bright pink light the craft appeared to be a metallic lead color. While the pink light seemed to be cloak the craft Meagan could see source from which the light may have come. From an opening they could see inside the craft. The same pink glow seemed to emanate from within.

Meagan would later describe the craft as being "egg-shaped from the top down", which appeared to have been cut straight across its bottom. At the bottom of the craft four thin, "spider like" legs supported it. A sucker pad at the bottom of each leg fixed it onto the road. Meagan estimated it as being around 12 feet high and 16 feet wide.

From their vantage point from the top of the embankment Meagan and Andre had a side on view of the object. Feeling more confused than afraid they quietly speculated that it could be some kind of experimental craft. As they continued to slowly approach the craft 5 or 6 men stepped out of the opening onto the ground. While one or two of the men, Andre and Meagan were never entirely sure which, disappeared from their view around the far side of the craft two of the men remained near its center, almost as if they were guarding it. The final two

men came to the side nearest to
Meagan and Andre.

The men were wearing identical suits,
which covered them from head to toe,
making it impossible for Meagan or
Andre to discern any muscles or other
defining features. Later Meagan would
say that she thought that the suits
were white but Andre saw them as
pink. With the exception of two of the
men, one on the far side and the one
nearest to Meagan and Andre, their
heads were also covered. The man
nearest Meagan and Andre had thick,
dark curly hair and a beard.

Meagan, standing on a slightly raised
embankment, had the impression of

looking down on them. Meagan was 5 foot 5 and the men came up to her chin. They were slender in build. Andre noted that one of the men on the far side bent down to pick up some sand from the ground on the side of the road before letting it trickle back down through his fingers.

Meagan and Andre described the two men nearest them as having a conversation. While one spoke in a high-pitched voice using singsong sounding words the other appeared monosyllabic in his answers. They could not hear actual words just the sound of the conversation. Meagan thought it sounded Chinese but found it too high pitched to accurately discern.

After a moment the man doing all the talking seemed to notice that Meagan and Andre were watching them. He said something to his companion. The bearded man turned to look at Meagan. His skin was olive, Middle Eastern in color. He bowed low, to the waist, and said something that Meagan took to be a greeting.

Throughout this exchange his eyes never left Meagan's. Despite this, and being quite sure that they were normal, Meagan had the impression that they were translucent as though she could look through them. Meagan felt herself drawn to him. She said hello before nervously laughing.

For the first time Meagan began to get the feeling that something was not right. She told Andre, who was now standing slightly behind his mother, to run home and get his father. Frightened, Andre didn't need to be asked twice.

As Meagan continued to stare at the men they conversed in monosyllables. Before she knew any time had passed they had returned to their craft. Meagan didn't remember seeing them board or the door closing.

Meagan became aware of a buzzing noise akin to a swarm of bees in a hive. The legs of the craft elongated to about three times their length raising the craft to an overall height of around 20 feet. Andre who had been making his way down the embankment stopped when he heard the buzzing sound. Meagan stepped back afraid of what was going to happen next.

The legs of the craft telescoped inside it as it hovered for a few seconds before shooting off into the night sky. The clouds were very low that night and Meagan could see the pink light shooting up into the clouds. While the craft disappeared in around 30 seconds the clouds seemed stained the same shade of pink for a while after.

Meagan was joined once again by Andre and they both stood there staring at the clouds, shocked. While they estimated that the episode lasted for around ten minutes it seemed much longer. Upon returning home Meagan decided not to wake her husband up as there was nothing he could do about it.

The next day no traces were found on the road.

Today while other similar encounters are far better known the Mindalore encounter is comparatively forgotten.

The Broad Haven Triangle

Following a spate of sightings across
the world in 1976 Welsh Ufologist
Randall Jones Pugh predicted that a
spate of events would follow in Wales
in the very near future. While not
many people took Jones' prediction
seriously even those who did found
what happened next to be
extraordinary.

Pembrokeshire in the south west of
Wales is one of the most picturesque
parts of the U.K. Much of its coastline,
including the town of Broad Haven,
forms the Pembrokeshire Coast
National Park. It was against this

prettiest of backdrops that the West Wales flap of 1977 occurred.

As they played in the playground of Broad Haven Primary School during lunchtime on the 4th of February 1977 a group of 15 schoolchildren claimed to see a silver cigar shaped UFO in the fields behind the school. Some of the children, aged between 9 and 11, also saw a silver man with pointed ears emerge from the craft. While the teachers and dinner ladies dismissed the story as fantasy, children are often prone to exaggeration and flights of fancy, so adamant were the children that after school had finished for the day they reported their sighting to the local police station.

The headmaster of the school, Ralph Llewellyn, had initially dismissed the pupil's claims, when they saw the craft some children had ran into the school to fetch the headmaster. Mr. Llewellyn annoyed that they were disturbing his lunch break, told them that he "couldn't be bothered to look" and sent the children back outside to play. Later, after learning of the visit to the police station, Llewellyn became intrigued by the children's persistence and asked them all to draw what they had seen. He was amazed at how similar their pictures were.

Just under two weeks later on the 17th of February teachers and dinner ladies at the school claimed to have seen the same craft in the field. One of the dinner ladies believed that she had seen a creature boarding the craft.

Encouraged by Randall Jones Pugh the story soon made its way into the national media. Journalists flocked to this remote part of the Welsh coast from all over Britain. UFOs and aliens quickly became the hot topic of discussion in Wales and by spring people were interpreting stars and planets in the sky as flying saucers and little green men. Some were even seeing silver humanoids wandering the countryside at night.

Sitting in an isolated position overlooking the dramatic Stack Rocks,

Ripperstone Farm was, at this time, home to dairyman Billy Coombs, his wife Pauline and their young children. It was here that much of the activity of the Broad Haven Triangle seemed to occur.

Over the space of a year the family experienced repeated encounters with strange crafts and unexplained lights. Often these encounters seemed to interfere with the family's electricity supply sending items haywire and electric bills spiraling. Pauline Coombs seemed to be the focus of the attention and claimed to be experiencing encounters on a monthly basis. Once the car she was driving was chased by a fiery, oval shaped object along the narrow county lanes.

Even more extraordinarily the couple claimed that one on occasion a herd of cows was teleported from a locked and secure field into an adjacent farmyard.

The most famous incident at Ripperstone farm was the appearance of a 7ft tall figure in a spacesuit whose blank face stared eerily through the living room windows. By the time the local police force had arrived there was no sign of the spaceman. The policeman who attended the farm later described them, as "the most frightened family I have ever been to see."

While much of the activity centered on Ripperstone Farm numerous sightings were reported all over the county. For example on the 13th of March a young boy named Steve Taylor claimed to have seen an orange, glowing disk in the sky. As he watched it a black dog ran past him.

Taylor followed the dog into a nearby field where he saw a large domed object. Next to it stood a tall man with high cheekbones, "like an old man", who was dressed in a one-piece suit. The man began to approach Taylor.

Frightened the teenager lashed out. Curiously his first punch hit nothing but air. Taylor fled. When he eventually got home the family dog growled at him as if he were a stranger.

At the same time, in nearby Milford Haven (around 8 miles from Broad Haven) a 17-year-old girl claimed to have seen a 3 ft. humanoid standing on her bedroom windowsill watching her.

Also in Milford Haven, on April the 7th Cyril John (64) had risen at 5:00 am to undertake a trip from his home to London. It was then that he saw a light shining into his bedroom window. On closer inspection John described it as an egg-shaped object, silver grey in color with an orangey- red light on the top of it.

The craft was around 4ft in diameter and seemed to rock gently in the air. Near it was a 7 or 8 ft. tall humanoid that John said was floating in mid-air like a "free-fall parachutist". The figure was dressed in a silver-grey suit with no visible facial features. Mr. John claimed that both the craft and spaceman seemingly hovered in the air motionless for around half an hour before moving slowly away.

Less than five minutes' drive from Broad Haven is the quaint village of

Little Haven. Here the owner of Haven Fort Hotel, Mrs. Rosa Glanville, reported that she was woken at 2:30 am on the 19th of April by a strange noise and lights outside. Looking out of her bedroom window Mrs. Glanville saw an object which she described as an "upside-down saucer" around the size "of a minibus" sitting in the field next to the hotel. 2 "faceless humanoids" with pointed heads were also in the field. Mrs. Glanville felt a heat so intense that she thought it was burning her face. The heat seemed to be coming from the multicolored flames, which were emanating from the craft.

As landlady of a famously haunted hotel Mrs. Glanville was not easily scared. She called out to the humanoids demanding to know what they were doing. Getting no response Mrs. Glanville went to rouse other residents of the hotel hoping that they could bear witness to the strange occurrence. When she returned to the window a few minutes later the field was empty.

With the encounter over Mrs. Glanville returned to bed. The next morning, remembering the events of the night before, Mrs. Glanville went to check the area where the craft had landed. There she found flattened grass and scorch-marks. Interestingly the landing site overlooked a field, which contained a Royal Observer Corps bunker.

Concerned Mrs. Glanville contacted her M.P., Nicholas Edwards, who in turn alerted the nearby RAF Brawdy air base. People from the base subsequently visited Mrs. Glanville and assured her that RAF Brawdy were not responsible for the events she had witnessed. They also urged her not to publicize the case as it might alarm the public. Sadly in the small community of Little Haven this was impossible, the story spread like wildfire.

Squadron Leader Tim Webb, who oversaw pilot training at Brawdy, confirmed that the "spacemen" people were describing did not match anything worn by base personnel. Interestingly Webb's son Michael was one of the children who say the UFO at Broad Haven Primary School. Webb told The Observer that he believed his son "implicitly" saying, "I've yet to see a UFO but I think there has to be something supernatural or paranormal."

It was during this period that the suggestion the spaceman was a worker from one of the local oil refineries wearing their protective suit was first put forward.

Back at Ripperstone Farm one incident stands above all the rest and the amount of witnesses to it mean it can't be easily dismissed. In June 1977 Mrs. Coombs returned from taking the children to a Silver Jubilee party to find her husband distressed and upset. He said that he had looked out of the window and noticed a strange silver car approaching the farmhouse.

In the car were two men in black suits. One got out of the car and approached the house. Feeling uneasy Billy had decided not to answer the door, instead pretending that nobody was home. The visit of the men to home of the Coombs family was witnessed by their next-door neighbor Caroline Klass, a nurse.

As Klass was putting rubbish in the outside bin one of the men appeared next to her. She described him as having strange, waxy skin with a high forehead, slicked back black hair and cold, unblinking eyes. In a thick foreign accent he asked where Mrs. Coombs was. Caroline Klass told him that she didn't know and quickly returned to her home.

Later that day Klass was talking to her friend Rosa Glanville of the Haven Fort Hotel. Mrs. Glanville told Klass that her daughter Anna, a student, had been alone in the hotel when a silver car had pulled up outside. The two men in black suits had entered the hotel and had asked for Mrs. Glanville by name. Anna sent them away but noticed that as they left their car made no noise on the gravel.

Despite RAF Brawdy claiming that the incidents had nothing to do with them and the MOD claiming to have "no record of unusual activity in the area" it seems that a discreet investigation was launched. Papers released a couple of years ago show that on the 14th of June 1977 the head of S4 (Air) (the MOD branch responsible for UFO sightings) asked the RAF Police to make discreet enquiries about the events in Wales.

Sadly no report on what the RAF investigation uncovered remains, if it has it will probably never be, released. However a secret briefing on UFO policy from December 1977 the head of S4 was quoted as saying that from time to time the public interest in UFOs increases, "there was some concern in Wales, although the RAF Police thought this could have been the work of a practical joker."

Indeed in 1996 Glyn Edwards a local businessman and member of the Milford Haven Round Table confessed that he had been responsible for the sightings of the 7ft spaceman. A silver lined asbestos suit borrowed from the local oil refinery with a solid in-built helmet was his costume. He and another member of the Round Table had come up with the idea after hearing of the encounter at Broad Haven Primary School.

Evans recalled that he had "visited the garden of a certain lady, who later called the police that I had to dive into a hedge because she appeared to be aiming a rifle or a shotgun at me."

While this accounts for at least some of the spaceman sightings other events are still unexplained. In 2015 Dave Davies, one of the schoolchildren who saw the original sighting, was interviewed by the Mirror newspaper. He said that despite the cynicism of others and the bullying that he had suffered he stood by what he saw that day. Many of his classmates feel the same way.

Local journalist Hugh Turnbull had reported the story for the Western Telegraph, the areas local newspaper. He believed that something military was behind the encounters. Others favored a more extreme solution, suggesting that aliens had an underground base beneath Stack Rocks in St Brides Bay. The claimed that UFOs were often seen to hover above the rocks before disappearing, supposedly diving under the water.

Another popular explanation was that despite official denials the range of military bases in the area was responsible. North of Broad Haven was a rocket testing station at Aberporth while Brawdy trained Hawker Hunter pilots and housed both a Tactical Weapons Unit and a US Navy underwater research station (later revealed to be a unit responsible for tracking the movements to Soviet submarines).

Interestingly when RAF Brawdy closed a few years ago, sceptics may have assumed that the UFOs would also leave the area. However this hasn't been the case. To this day cigar-shaped UFOs are seen in the area.

Despite attempts by journalist Ray Gosling to debunk the sightings in the area many witnesses still stick doggedly to their stories. It seems that the truth of the Broad Haven Triangle is yet to be revealed.

Kelly Cahill

The Kelly Cahill encounter is possibly Australia's most well-known Alien encounter.

The Cahill family was an ordinary Australian family living in the Melbourne suburb of Belgrave. As the clock approached midnight on August the 8th 1993 the Cahills- Kelly, her husband and their three children, were driving home through the Dandenong foothills after visiting friends. It was then that they noticed the lights of a rounded craft in the sky above them.

The craft seemed to hover silently above the road. The family observed that different colored lights were discernible on the bottom of the object. Kelly Cahill later stated that it was so close to the ground she thought she could see people looking out of its windows. Suddenly the craft zoomed away, disappearing as quickly as it had appeared.

The family continued their journey home keeping one eye on the sky in case they should see it again. It was then that they were practically blinded by an intense bright light. Frightened by the light Kelly's husband kept driving, desperate to get his family to safety.

As they sped away Kelly found herself feeling very relaxed as if the disappearance of the light was reassuring. She thought she might have blacked out but when asking her husband if she had he didn't respond.

Upon their arrival home Kelly could smell a foul odor, like vomit and began to sense that something was missing. What was missing was an hour of their journey.

Later, as Kelly undressed for bed, she noticed a strange triangular mark on her naval.

That night Kelly dreamt that she was back at the site of the encounter. As she sits at the side of the road she sees her husband being led out of the craft by a creature that Kelly assumes is female. She tackles the creature before blacking out.

Kelly then finds herself on the far right of the field away from the UFO. Next to her is a body, which seems to take on a human form. A middle-aged woman is repeatedly screaming "Murderess" at her. Kelly finds herself overcome with grief, unaware that she has killed anybody.

A hand is placed on Kelly's shoulder. She is led into the craft and soon finds herself in a small room. In it, next to a table, stood one of the creatures. The creature tells her she hasn't killed anyone, it explains that they were using her sense of morality to overcome her fear. For some reason Kelly thinks that she knows this creature.

Also in the room is a Bible belonging to Kelly, it had disappeared from the family home a few weeks previously. The creature then gives Kelly a choice: she can come with them but must leave the Bible behind. The dream ends with the creature giving Kelly the bible.

A few days after the encounter Kelly's husband found the missing Bible in the family car.

For the next few weeks Kelly suffered from what she described as a general malaise and was hospitalized twice, once for severe stomach pain and the second time for a uterine infection. It was during this period that she began to remember further details from the night.

Kelly recalled a large UFO, around 150 feet in diameter, hovering above a gully. She also remembered that the first time they saw it her husband had stopped the car and they had both walked towards it. Kelly remembered feeling calm but afraid. She felt as though they were being drawn to the craft. She also remembered that on the opposite side of the road another car had stopped to look at it.

As the Cahills approached the craft they saw a creature Kelly described as black, "not a black color but black as if all matter was removed". She thought it was soulless. It was around seven feet tall with large red eyes, which glowed in the night.

After a moment Kelly noticed that there were "heaps" of these creatures all in the open field beneath their craft. They appeared to be in small groups, one of which glided towards Kelly and her husband covering the distance effortlessly in only a matter of seconds.

In the distance a second group of creatures approached the other car.

Kelly recalled feeling that the creatures were evil and that she had clung to her husband for protection, fighting the urge to black out. Kelly's next memory was of being back in the family car.

Further dreams led to Kelly recalling much of what happened that night.

In many of the dreams she sensed a presence, which warns her to be calm, however Kelly felt it had a sinister motive. Later on she would experience her legs being lifted and drawn out of the bed. Again the presence was present. In the dreams

Kelly eventually sees the creature leaning over her, about to kiss her naval.

Conversely Kelly's husband recalls hardly anything of that night. While he remembers the UFO he does not recall stopping the car or the alien creatures.

With her husband unable to remember and unwilling to discuss events Kelly felt increasingly isolated. As she struggled to make sense of the encounter Kelly contacted various universities and aviation authorities. Despite her extensive attempts Kelly was unable to find any satisfactory answers to what she experienced that night.

Unlike many other encounters the Cahill experience is not without corroboration. As well as the car that Kelly had seen a third car was parked further up the road with its lights off. According to the occupants of car two, Bill, Jane and Glenda, the third car contained one visible occupant- a man who was gazing fixedly toward the UFO.

Both Jane and Glenda were able to recall being on the craft. Like Kelly they described the creatures as being tall and black. Unlike Kelly they did not describe them as having red eyes.

The women did not think that they were abducted instead feeling as if they exercised free will throughout.

Curiously while the women didn't remember seeing each other while on board the craft each was aware of what was happening to her companion.

Much of what Kelly experienced also occurred to both Jane and Glenda. Unlike Kelly neither Jane nor Glenda suffered any after affects.

Like Kelly's husband, Bill seems to have had only a limited role in the encounter. While he was able, with the help of hypnosis, to recall smells, sounds and the sense of activity Bill does not have any visual memories of the encounter.

That Jane, Glenda and Bill experienced a strikingly similar encounter to the Cahills adds credence to the case. This is further enhanced by the fact that neither group knew each other and was unable to discuss their encounter with each other before being interviewed.

Ufologists later visited the site of the encounter and found a possible related ground trace and low-level magnetic anomaly at the encounter site.

Today some consider Kelly Cahills encounter to be an elaborate hoax. While parts may have been exaggerated or invented in the constant retelling the story is yet to be disapproved. Kelly Cahill was considered to be a reliable, honest person by those who knew her and had no reason to invent the story.

Printed in Great Britain
by Amazon

62466886R00076